CAMP
B
F
F

CAMP

BY KAYLA MILLER

HOUGHTON MIFFLIN HARCOURT
BOSTON NEW YORK

Additional color by Miguel Co

hmhbooks.com

The illustrations in this book were done using inks and digital color.
The text type was set in Kayla Miller's handwriting.
The display type was hand-lettered by Kayla Miller.

Design by Andrea Miller

ISBN: 978-1-328-53081-3 hardcover
ISBN: 978-1-328-53082-0 paperback

Printed in the United States of America
DOC 10 9 8 7 6 5 4 3 2 1
4500751315

FOR GRANDMA -KM

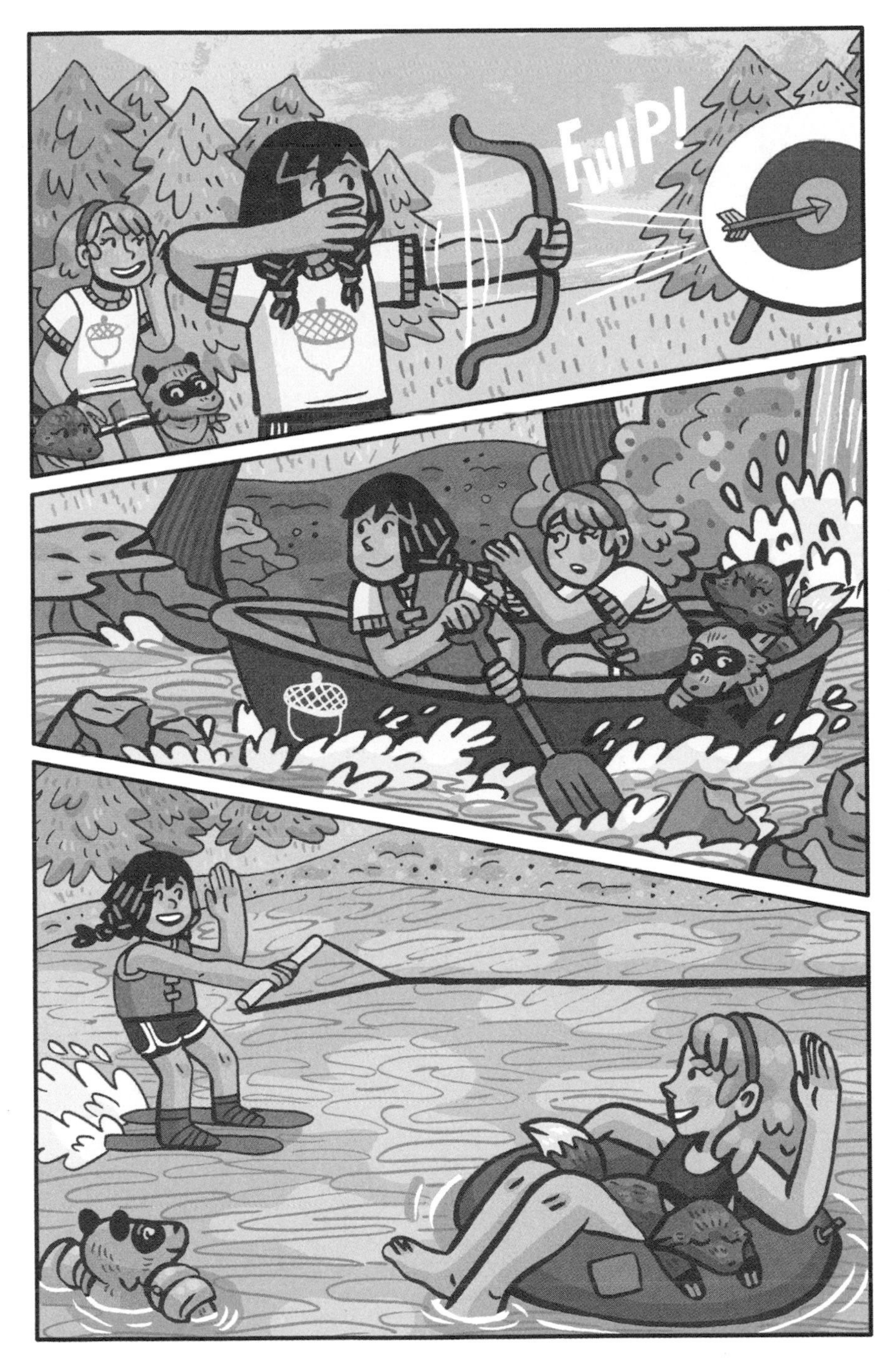
FWIP!

OLIVE!
EARTH TO OLIVE!
ARE YOU LISTENING?

HUH?
YOU WERE SLEEPING WITH YOUR EYES OPEN.
YOU LOOKED LIKE A ZOMBIE.
I'M JUST NOT USED TO BEING UP THIS EARLY IN THE SUMMER.
I WISH THE CAMP BUS LEFT A LITTLE LATER.
I HAD TO GET UP TOO... AND I'M NOT EVEN GOING TO CAMP, SO STAY AWAKE AND ANSWER MY QUESTION!
WHAT IS IT, GOOBER?
I **ASKED**:

CAN I HAVE YOUR SKATEBOARD IF YOU GET EATEN BY A BEAR?
I'M NOT GOING TO GET EATEN.
BUT IF I DID...
I'D COME BACK AS A GHOST AND HAUNT YOU IF YOU EVEN THINK ABOUT TAKING MY STUFF!
THERE AREN'T REALLY ANY BEARS AT CAMP, ARE THERE?
MAYBE...BUT THE COUNSELORS PROBABLY WOULDN'T LET THEM EAT ANY KIDS.

SWEET PEA, I'VE PACKED YOUR INHALER IN THE FRONT POCKET OF YOUR BACKPACK...
OKAY.
AND WE ALREADY MAILED YOUR ALLERGY MEDICINE TO THE CAMP NURSE-
BUT YOU HAVE TO REMEMBER TO GO TO HER AND TAKE IT EVERY NIGHT AFTER DINNER.
OKAY, MOMMA. I KNOW.
AND I PACKED YOU AN EXTRA TOOTHBRUSH IN CASE SOMETHING HAPPENS TO THE ONE IN YOUR TRAVEL CASE.
AND YOU HAVE A PACK OF NASAL STRIPS SO YOU WON'T KEEP THE OTHER KIDS UP IF YOU SNORE.

DADDY AND I PACKED YOU PLENTY OF STATIONERY SO YOU CAN WRITE HOME AS MUCH AS YOU WANT IF YOU START TO FEEL LONELY...
AND ALL OF OUR EMERGENCY NUMBERS ARE WRITTEN ON THE INSIDE COVER OF YOUR NOTEBOOK IF YOU NEED TO CALL US...
AND WE'RE ONLY AN HOUR AND A HALF AWAY IF YOU NEED US TO COME GET YOU, PUMPKIN.
YOU KNOW, MISTY, I DON'T THINK YOU HAVE TO WORRY QUITE SO MUCH.
WE REQUESTED THAT THE GIRLS BE PUT IN THE SAME BUNK SO THEY COULD TAKE CARE OF EACH OTHER WHILE THEY'RE AWAY.
RIGHT, GUYS?
YEAH!
RIGHT!

I CAN'T WAIT TO SEE THE CAMP! THE MAP ONLINE MADE IT LOOK HUGE.
YEAH! I'M GLAD THAT THE CABINS ARE CLOSE TO THE ARTS AND CRAFTS BUILDING.
I WISH WE WERE A LITTLE CLOSER TO THE SPORTS FIELDS... BUT I GUESS WALKING WILL BE A NICE WARM-UP.
I HOPE WE CAN TAKE ALL OF THE CLASSES WE WANT TO TAKE... THE SCHEDULING SEEMS A LITTLE MORE CONFUSING THAN AT SCHOOL.
I HAVE A FEW ACTIVITIES I **REALLY** WANNA DO, BUT THERE ARE A TON OF COOL ONES.
I GUESS WE'LL FIND OUT WHEN WE GET THERE.
IT'S NOT FAIR! HOW COME LIV GETS TO GO TO CAMP AND I DON'T!?
YOU'RE TOO YOUNG, SWEETHEART. YOU CAN GO WHEN YOU'RE OLIVE'S AGE.
I PROMISE AUNT MOLLY AND I WILL TAKE YOU SOMEWHERE FUN THIS WEEKEND.

LIBRARY
LIBRARY
OLIVE

OFFICE
CAMP ACORN LAKE

YOU'RE THE NEW BUNNY BUNKERS, WILLOW AND OLIVE, RIGHT?
YOU GUYS CAN GO WAIT BY THE SIGN THAT SAYS "BUNNY" ON IT AND I'LL JOIN YOU ONCE I HAVE THE REST OF THE BUS SORTED.
CAMP ACORN
OLIVE
WHOA THERE, TOUGH STUFF!
I LIKE YOUR ATTITUDE, BUT WE TYPICALLY BRING THE BAGS TO THE CABINS ON A GOLF CART. IT'S A BIT OF A HIKE.
THANKS!
CAMP ACORN LAKE
170
FOX
BUNNY

BUNNY
HEY, GUYS!
HELLO, EVERYONE.
CAMP ACORN LAKE
HEY, ASHLEY!
OH MY GOSH! I MISSED YOU, LAURA!
OKAY,
WE HAVE CECILY,
ROSIE,
LESLIE,
BREE,
VANESSA,
CHRIS,
ELLEN,
AIDY...
AND OUR TWO NEW RECRUITS—
WILLOW AND OLIVE!
WELCOME TO CAMP ACORN LAKE!
THANKS.

SINCE WE'RE ALL ACCOUNTED FOR, HOW ABOUT WE GO FOR A WALK AROUND CAMP BEFORE HEADING TO THE CABIN?
I KNOW I WANT TO STRETCH MY LEGS AFTER THAT BUS RIDE!
CAMP ACORN LAKE
OLIVE, WILLOW,
WHY DON'T YOU COME UP HERE AND WE'LL GIVE YOU A GUIDED TOUR?
OKAY, SO, THE BUSES DROPPED US OFF IN FRONT OF THE MAIN OFFICE... AND I DON'T THINK YOU NEED ME TO POINT OUT WHERE THE LAKE IS.
CAMP ACORN LAKE

HERE ARE THE SPORTS FIELDS! WE HAVE TENNIS, BASKETBALL, SOCCER, SOFTBALL...
AND THE GYM, WHERE WE STORE EQUIPMENT AND HAVE ACROBATICS ACTIVITIES.
CAMP
AND OVER HERE IS THE THEATER, WHERE WE PUT ON PLAYS...
AND THE TUNE SHACK FOR MUSIC PRACTICES.
CAMP ACORN
THIS IS ONE OF MY FAVORITE BUILDINGS AT CAMP: THE MESS HALL!
MESS HALL
AND THERE'S THE INFIRMARY.
WILLOW, YOUR SHEET SAYS YOU TAKE MEDICATION, SO WE SHOULD TALK ABOUT THE NURSE'S OFFICE LATER.
CAMP ACORN

THAT'S MY FAVORITE BUILDING: THE ART BARN! THAT'S WHERE ALL OF THE ARTS AND CRAFTS ACTIVITIES TAKE PLACE.
AND THOSE OTHER BUILDINGS ARE FOR VIDEO, MAGIC, AND SCIENCE... YOU KNOW, INDOOR-KID ACTIVITIES.
BARN
INDOOR-KID?
YEAH... IT'S JUST CAMP-SPEAK FOR PEOPLE WHO DON'T LIKE SPORTS.
CAMP ACORN LAKE
AND WAAAY OVER THERE IS THE SKATE PARK!
COOL!
THERE'S THE NATURE SHED AND THE FOREST TRAIL.
WHICH IS JUST ABOUT ALL THERE IS, ASIDE FROM...

THE CABINS!
WHOA!

I WANT TO BUNK WITH YOU, LAURA!
I WANT A TOP BUNK!
I CALL CORNER!
YOU WANNA SHARE A BUNK, RIGHT?
OF COURSE!
CAN I HAVE THE LOWER BUNK?
YEAH—I WANTED TOP BUNK ANYWAY!

IT LOOKS GREAT IN HERE, GUYS!
I WORKED UP AN APPETITE JUST WATCHING YOU GUYS BUZZ AROUND.
YOU COULD WORK UP AN APPETITE WATCHING THE INSIDES OF YOUR EYELIDS...
BUT YOU'RE IN LUCK BECAUSE IT HAPPENS TO BE LUNCHTIME.
MESS HALL

IT SMELLS GREAT IN HERE!
THE COOK IS AMAZING.
I WASN'T KIDDING YOU WHEN I SAID THIS WAS MY FAVORITE PLACE AT CAMP.
CAMP ACORN
I DON'T REALLY LIKE MEATLOAF...
THAT'S OKAY, IT'S NOT MY FAVORITE EITHER.
CAMP ACORN
MAY WE HAVE TWO PLATES WITH NO MEATLOAF BUT EXTRA MAC AND VEGGIES?
CAMP

QUIET, EVERYONE!! QUIET!
AFTER EVERYONE HAS CLEANED UP THEIR DISHES, PLEASE RETURN TO YOUR TABLES AS WE'LL BE HANDING OUT THE ACTIVITY SIGN-UP SHEETS.
PLEASE NEATLY PRINT YOUR NAME AND BUNK AT THE TOP.
THE ACTIVITIES ARE GROUPED INTO SIX TIME SLOTS— YOU MAY CIRCLE ONE ACTIVITY PER HOUR. IF YOU NEGLECT TO CIRCLE AN ACTIVITY, I WILL CIRCLE ONE FOR YOU AT RANDOM AND YOU WILL NOT BE ABLE TO CHANGE IT UNTIL WE SELECT ACTIVITIES AGAIN NEXT WEEK.
IF YOU HAVE ANY QUESTIONS ABOUT THE ACTIVITIES LISTED, PLEASE ASK YOUR COUNSELORS.

SPORTS
ART
MUSIC
SCIENCE
WHAT ACTIVITIES DO YOU THINK WE SHOULD TRY?

I'M THINKING...PAINTING, VIDEO, NATURE EXPLORATION, SOFTBALL, SKATE PARK, AND... JEWELRY MAKING?
DOES THAT SOUND GOOD?
WELL...I LIKE PAINTING, AND NATURE, AND JEWELRY... VIDEO SOUNDS OKAY SO LONG AS I DON'T HAVE TO GET IN FRONT OF THE CAMERA...
...BUT I DON'T KNOW HOW TO PLAY SOFTBALL, OR SKATEBOARD ...AND I REALLY WANTED TO TAKE A MAGIC CLASS.
OKAY...WELL, SOFTBALL IS REALLY EASY—IF YOU WANT TO GIVE IT A TRY, I CAN HELP YOU. AND I'LL TRY MAGIC...
HOW ABOUT WE TAKE BEGINNER'S SLEIGHT OF HAND MAGIC INSTEAD OF GOING TO THE SKATE PARK?
OKAY...

CAMP ACORN LAKE
CAMP ACORN LAKE
LET'S PLAY SOME ICEBREAKER GAMES TO WELCOME OUR NEW BUNNY BUNK GIRLS!
WE COULD PLAY THE GUMMY GAME! BUT, WE HAVE TO PLAY OUTSIDE BECAUSE—
"NO EATING IN THE CABIN!"
WE KNOW, LAURA!

OKAY, SO FOR THIS GAME WE'RE GOING TO PASS THIS PACK OF CANDY AROUND IN A CIRCLE, AND WHEN IT'S YOUR TURN YOU TAKE ONE PIECE WITHOUT LOOKING.
EACH COLOR REPRESENTS A DIFFERENT CATEGORY.
RED IS FAVORITE HOBBY,
ORANGE IS FAVORITE SUBJECT IN SCHOOL,
GREEN IS WHAT YOU WANT TO BE WHEN YOU GROW UP,
AND BLUE IS RANDOM FACT!
ON YOUR TURN, YOU TELL US YOUR NAME AND THEN GIVE YOUR ANSWER FOR THE COLOR YOU CHOSE...
AND THEN EAT THE CANDY, OF COURSE!
FOR EXAMPLE— I'M LAURA AND MY FAVORITE ANIMAL IS THE SEA TURTLE!

MY NAME IS ELLEN AND MY FAVORITE SUBJECT IS MATH!
I'M ROSIE AND MY FAVORITE HOBBY IS COLLECTING SHELLS.
MY NAME IS VANESSA AND I CAN NAME EVERY STATE CAPITAL.
HEY, I'M BREE AND MY HOBBY IS MAKING COSTUMES WITH MY OLDER SISTER!
I'M THE ONE AND ONLY CECILY AND I WANT TO BE A MOVIE STAR WHEN I GROW UP.
MY NAME IS CHRISTINA, BUT YOU CAN CALL ME CHRIS, AND MY FAVORITE SUBJECT IN SCHOOL IS...HMM...SCIENCE.
HI, I'M AIDY. WHEN I GROW UP I WANT TO BE A MARINE BIOLOGIST.
MY NAME IS LESLIE AND MY FAVORITE SUBJECT IS READING.
UM... HI...
I'M WILLOW...
AND... UM...

I AM...
UMMM...
I LIKE...
I DUNNO...
WILLOW, WHY DON'T YOU TELL US YOUR FAVORITE TIME OF YEAR?
CAMP
MY NAME IS WILLOW, AND MY FAVORITE SEASON IS FALL!
CAMP ACORN LAKE

OH COOL.
MY NAME IS OLIVE AND I HAVE A LOT OF FAVORITE HOBBIES...
BUT I GUESS MY ABSOLUTE FAVORITES ARE DRAWING,
READING,
SOFTBALL,
SKATEBOARDING,
AND WATCHING SCARY MOVIES!
THE WHOLE IDEA OF FAVORITES IS YOU CAN ONLY PICK ONE, GOOFBALL.
I LIKE THEM ALL EQUALLY!
I'M ASHLEY AND WHEN I GROW UP—ERR—MORE THAN I ALREADY HAVE—I WANT TO BE A PHYSICAL THERAPIST.

CAMP
ACORN

RISE AND SHINE, CAMP ACORN LAKE!
IT'S A BEAUTIFUL DAY!
OFFICE
YAWN
COME ON, BUNNIES! BREAKFAST IS IN THIRTY MINUTES!
NNN

COOL SHIRT, OLIVE!
THANKS— MY AUNT GOT IT FOR ME!
UM... BREE, RIGHT?
YUP, THAT'S ME!
GOTTA GO MAKE MY BED BEFORE BREAKFAST OR LAURA WILL COMPLAIN.

DOES EVERYONE KNOW WHERE THEY'RE GOING FOR THEIR FIRST ACTIVITY?
YES.
UH-HUH.
WILLOW, OLIVE, YOUR FIRST ACTIVITY IS IN THE ART BARN, SO YOU CAN FOLLOW ME.
OKAY!
ART BARN

VIDEO
OKAY, BREE, SO YOU SIT HERE AND I'LL BE THE WAITRESS.
OH! CAN I BE THE FANCY GUY WHO SEATS PEOPLE?
I CAN DO A POSH FRENCH ACCENT!
THAT SOUNDS GREAT, MAX!
WHO DO YOU WANT TO BE, WILLOW?
I'VE GOT TO WORK THE CAMERA.
I COULD GO GET A TRIPOD SO YOU COULD BE IN THE SCENE TOO!

No!
I'D...REALLY RATHER WORK THE CAMERA.
OKAY.

OLIVE, WILLOW, YOU GIRLS ARE DOING SOFTBALL, RIGHT?
CHRIS HERE IS KIND OF OUR STAR PITCHER.
REALLY?
YEAH. I PITCH FOR MY TEAM AT HOME, TOO.
AWESOME! I PLAY SECOND BASE ON MY TEAM AT HOME.
HOW ARE YOU AT BAT?
I'M OKAY... I HAVE A PROBLEM WITH INSIDE PITCHES SOMETIMES.
YOU SHOULD LET THE COACH KNOW SO WE CAN WORK ON IT.

HEADS UP, WILLOW!
HIT THE CUT OFF!
HUH?
JUST PICK IT UP AND THROW IT TO ME!

OKAY, DOES ANYONE KNOW HOW TO DO THE "REVERSED CARD" TRICK?
I'D LOVE TO HAVE SOMEONE HELP ME SHOW THE GROUP.
I'VE SEEN YOU DO THIS ONE BEFORE. YOU SHOULD GO UP!
YEAH, BUT... LET'S JUST LET THE COUNSELOR DO IT, OKAY?

I THINK I WANT GREEN...
I REALLY LIKE THIS BLUE, AND THIS PINK...
AND THIS PURPLE.
OOOH, CAN YOU PUT THAT PURPLE IN MINE, TOO? THAT WAY WE'LL MATCH.
I'M GLAD YOU HAVE A SMALL WRIST...
BECAUSE THIS SEEMS LIKE IT'S GOING TO TAKE FOREVER.
IT'LL BE WORTH IT BECAUSE I'LL WEAR IT FOREVER.

WE'RE SETTING UP A NAIL SALON ON THE PORCH. DO YOU WANT TO GET YOUR NAILS DONE?
YEAH! DO YOU HAVE PURPLE?

YEAH, I THINK WE HAVE TWO PURPLES, AND ROSIE HAS A PEN THAT CAN DRAW ON TOP OF THE POLISH...
C'MON, WILLOW!
I'M NOT REALLY IN THE MOOD TO PAINT NAILS... YOU GUYS CAN GO WITHOUT ME.

UM...
LAURA?
HELLO, WILLOW.
WHAT'S UP?
I WAS WONDERING... COULD I GO CALL MY MOM?
I'M SORRY, WILLOW.
BUT CALLS HOME ARE FOR EMERGENCIES ONLY.
IF YOU'RE MISSING YOUR MOM YOU COULD WRITE HER A POSTCARD. I WANTED TO SEND SOME CARDS TO MY FRIENDS FROM SCHOOL, SO WHY DON'T WE WRITE TOGETHER?
OKAY...

ARE YOU FEELING OKAY?
YEAH, I'M FINE...
GOOD NIGHT, WILLOW.
G'NIGHT, OLIVE...

HEY, OLIVE, WOULD YOU MIND BRAIDING MY HAIR? IT LOOKS LIKE IT'S GONNA BE HOT TODAY AND I WANT MY HAIR OUT OF MY FACE.
SURE!
THANKS!

WILL YOU BRAID MY HAIR NEXT, OLIVE?
HUH? YOU NEVER WEAR YOUR HAIR IN A BRAID.
WELL, TODAY I WANT TO. COULD YOU GIVE ME TWINTAILS JUST LIKE YOU HAVE?
UH, OKAY.

DIRECTOR
FREE
HRUGS
5

WILLOW, WHY DON'T I PAIR YOU UP WITH ONE OF THE OTHER CAMPERS WHILE I HELP OLIVE WITH THIS TRICK?
NO! I WANT TO STAY WITH OLIVE.

ALMOST...
OLIVE!
DONE!
WOW!

THOSE FRIENDSHIP BRACELETS ARE COOL. DID YOU MAKE THEM?
YEAH! I COULD MAKE YOU ONE TOO, IF YOU WANT...
REALLY?!
WHAT COLORS DO YOU WANT?
UMM... YELLOW AND... RED AND...

ARE YOU OKAY, WILLOW?
YOU HAVEN'T EATEN MUCH TODAY.
I DON'T REALLY LIKE THIS FOOD...
HOW ABOUT WE MAKE YOU A SUNFLOWER BUTTER SANDWICH? IT TASTES JUST LIKE PEANUT BUTTER AND IT TASTES EVEN BETTER WITH BANANA SLICES ON IT.
OKAY...

FREE SHRUGS
HEY, GUYS!
WHO WANTS TO PLAY WACKY WORDS?
WACKY WORDS

OKAY!
CAN I WRITE FIRST?
COUNT ME IN.
YEAH!
FREE SHRUGS
YOU'RE NOT GONNA PLAY?
NO...
...I WANT TO WRITE A LETTER TO MY PARENTS.
DIDN'T YOU WRITE HOME LAST NIGHT?
YOU SHOULD COME HANG WITH US!
I...REALLY JUST WANT TO WRITE MY LETTER.
FREE SHRUGS

AN ADJECTIVE?
SLIMY!
AND A TYPE OF ANIMAL?
PANDA.

AN ADVERB?
SWIFTLY.
A TIME OF DAY?
THE WITCHING HOUR!
OOOH, NICE!
UM, OLIVE?
WILLOW! ARE YOU GOING TO PLAY?
NO... I JUST FINISHED MY LETTER AND I WANTED TO KNOW IF YOU'D WANT TO COME SIT WITH ME AND DRAW?

IT'S ALMOST MY TURN TO WRITE...
PLEASE?
WHY DON'T YOU PLAY A ROUND WITH US SO I CAN HAVE MY TURN WRITING AND THEN WE CAN GO DRAW?
NO.
IT'S FINE.
WHATEVER.
NEVER MIND.

AN ADJEC—
YAWN
OKAY, I GUESS IT'S TIME TO GET READY FOR BED, HUH?
FREE SHRUGS
HEY.
HMPH.

GOOD NIGHT, WILLOW.
YEAH.

HUH?

WILLOW?
OLIVE!
C'MON, OLIVE!
TWANG!

LET'S GO, WILLOW.
HURRY, OLIVE!

WILLOW, PLEASE!
COME ON!
C'MON!
WILLOW...
WHAT'S WRONG?
WHY ARE YOU CRYING?
TALK TO ME.
WILLOW...
PLEASE...

GASP!
WILLOW?

ASHLEY!
I WOKE UP AND WILLOW WASN'T IN HER BED AND I DON'T KNOW WHERE SHE IS.

IT'S OKAY, WE KNOW WHERE SHE IS.
WILLOW WAS HAVING A HARD TIME SLEEPING... SO SHE'S SITTING OUTSIDE WITH LAURA FOR A BIT.
CAN I GO OUTSIDE AND CHECK ON HER?
YEAH... I THINK THAT'S A NICE IDEA.

IT'S OKAY, SWEETIE...
IT'S ALL RIGHT.
WILLOW?
OLIVE?
ARE YOU OKAY?
I'M JUST FEELING A LITTLE HOMESICK.

HOMESICK?
BUT WE'VE ONLY BEEN HERE FOR A FEW DAYS...
SOMETIMES THE FIRST FEW DAYS ARE THE HARDEST.
IT CAN BE A BIG ADJUSTMENT BEING AWAY FROM HOME FOR THE FIRST TIME.
IF YOU'RE HAVING A ROUGH TIME, WE'LL WORK THROUGH IT TOGETHER.

RISE AND SHINE, CAMPERS!
OFFI
YAWN
ARE YOU FEELING OKAY?

HUH? OH, I'M JUST A LITTLE TIRED.
ONLY A LITTLE?
LOOKS LIKE YOU'RE GOING TO NEED SOME EXTRA SYRUP ON YOUR PANCAKES THIS MORNING, OLLIE.
OLLIE?
YEAH! DO YOU MIND IF I CALL YOU THAT?

NO.
I LIKE IT!
WELL, I DON'T.
EVERYONE AT HOME EITHER CALLS HER OLIVE OR LIV.
NO ONE CALLS HER **OLLIE**.
AT HOME EVERYONE CALLS ME TINA BUT HERE THEY CALL ME CHRIS.
IT'S LIKE A CAMP NICKNAME.

WE COULD GIVE YOU A NICKNAME TOO!
HOW ABOUT WILL... OR LOW OR—
NO, THANK YOU.
OKAY, GIRLS, BREAKFAST TIME!

MILK

AMP

OOPS, I FORGOT MY MEDICATION.
I'M GOING TO GO TO THE NURSE.
I'LL BE BACK IN A SECOND.
UH-HUH.
HEY, OLIVE.

OH, HEY, LAURA.
ARE YOU FEELING ALL RIGHT?
YEAH, I'M FINE...
YOU'VE SEEMED A LITTLE OFF ALL DAY.
I DIDN'T KNOW YOU COULD **BE** SO QUIET.

DID YOU WANT TO TALK ABOUT ANYTHING?
WELL...
I DON'T KNOW...
I'VE BEEN TRYING TO SPEND MORE TIME WITH WILLOW SINCE, YOU KNOW, LAST NIGHT.
I WANT HER TO FEEL BETTER AND NOT MISS HOME SO MUCH...
BUT SHE ALWAYS WANTS IT TO BE JUST THE TWO OF US, NO ONE ELSE, ALL DAY.
EVEN THOUGH THE OTHER KIDS ARE TRYING TO GET TO KNOW HER!
IT'S KIND OF DRIVING ME CRAZY...

I THINK IT'S REALLY NICE THAT YOU'RE TRYING TO BE THERE FOR YOUR FRIEND...
BUT WILLOW'S HAPPINESS ISN'T YOUR RESPONSIBILITY.
IT'S GREAT THAT YOU'RE HERE FOR HER IF SHE NEEDS TO TALK AND THAT YOU WANT TO SPEND TIME WITH HER...
BUT IF YOU'RE MAKING YOURSELF MISERABLE TRYING TO CHEER HER UP, THAT'S JUST SOLVING A PROBLEM BY CREATING A NEW ONE, ISN'T IT?

I JUST WISH SHE'D OPEN UP TO MY OTHER FRIENDS SO WE COULD ALL HANG OUT TOGETHER.
GIVE HER A LITTLE WHILE TO WARM UP TO EVERYONE...
AND IN THE MEANTIME, DON'T FEEL LIKE YOU'RE BEING SELFISH IF YOU DON'T PUT HER NEEDS BEFORE YOUR OWN ONE HUNDRED PERCENT OF THE TIME.
YOU CAN BE A SUPPORTIVE FRIEND TO WILLOW AND STILL TAKE TIME TO HANG OUT WITH YOUR OTHER FRIENDS AND DO THE THINGS YOU WANT TO DO, OKAY?
YEAH.

LAURA!
HEY, JAY.
I'M GLAD I RAN INTO YOU.
ASH SAID SHE WASN'T SURE WHERE YOU WERE.
JAY, HAVE YOU MET OLIVE YET?
SHE'S ONE OF MY NEW CAMPERS.
NICE TO MEET YOU, OLIVE.
I'M JAY.
I TEACH GUITAR AT THE TUNE SHACK.
YOU PLAY GUITAR?

YEAH, AND DRUMS.
THAT'S SO COOL!
IF YOU'RE INTERESTED IN LEARNING AN INSTRUMENT, I COULD GIVE YOU A QUICK LESSON DURING FREE HOUR.
THAT WOULD BE AWESOME!
COOL. I'LL MEET YOU AT THE TUNE SHACK IN A BIT, AFTER I FINISH TALKING TO LAURA.

CAN I BRING A FRIEND?
YEAH, OF COURSE.
COME ON, WILLOW.
WHERE ARE WE GOING?
THE TUNE SHACK.
WE HAVE A MUSIC LESSON!

ROCK!
HEY, GUYS, HOPE YOU WEREN'T WAITING TOO LONG.
NOT AT ALL!

SO YOU'RE BOTH HERE TO TRY GUITAR?
YEAH!
WELL, I AM.
I THINK WILLOW IS JUST HERE TO LISTEN.

I THINK YOUR POINTER FINGER SLID OUT OF PLACE.
TRY TO KEEP IT RIGHT ABOVE THE FRET.
OKAY.

IF YOU'RE GOING TO SIT AT THE DRUM SET, YOU MIGHT AS WELL TRY PLAYING A LITTLE.
IT'S NOT AS HARD AS IT LOOKS, I PROMISE.
IT'S MAINLY ABOUT KEEPING A BEAT.
TRY HITTING THE HI-HAT ONCE ON EVERY NUMBER AND ONCE BETWEEN EACH NUMBER, OKAY?
...OKAY.
ONE AND TWO AND
THREE AND FOUR AND-
ONE AND TWO AND
THREE AND FOUR AND-
TING-TING-TING-TING-

GREAT! NOW HIT THE SNARE DRUM WITH YOUR OTHER STICK ON TWO AND FOUR.
ONE AND TWO AND
THREE AND FOUR AND—
ONE AND TWO AND
THREE AND FOUR AND—
TING
BUM!
TING
TING-
BUM!
WOW! THAT ACTUALLY SOUNDS LIKE PART OF A SONG!
IT COULD BE IF SHE KEEPS PRACTICING!

THAT WAS FUN!
YEAH.
IF EITHER OF YOU WANT TO TAKE MORE LESSONS, LET ME KNOW AND I'LL FIT YOU INTO THE SCHEDULE.
OKAY.
THANK YOU.
GOOD NIGHT, JAY!

OLLIE AND WILLOW ARE BACK!
WANNA PLAY GO FISH WITH US UNTIL LIGHTS OUT?
I WAS HOPING WE COULD READ BEFORE BED...
MAYBE NEXT TIME.
OKAY.
good night
good night

G'NIGHT, WILLOW.
GOOD NIGHT, OLIVE.
RUSTLE
RUSTLE
HMM...

TOSS
TURN
MMM...

WAKE UP, BUNNIES!
DO YOU KNOW WHAT DAY IT IS?
UHHHH—
IT'S HALFWAY DAY!
MY FAVORITE DAY OF CAMP!
WHERE WE CELEBRATE MAKING IT HALFWAY THROUGH THE CAMP SESSION BY PLAYING GAMES ALL DAY AND HAVING A BIG ICE CREAM SOCIAL AT NIGHT!
SO EVERYONE GET UP, UP, UP!
AND WEAR SOMETHING GOLD!
THAT'S OUR BUNK'S COLOR THIS YEAR, AND I WANT EVERYONE TO KNOW IT'S BUNNY BUNK KICKING THEIR BUTTS AT TUG OF WAR!

OKAY, FIRST WE HAVE SPOON RACES AGAINST SKUNK BUNK!
LET'S SHOW THEM WHAT WE'VE GOT!
WHOO! YEAH!
UM, LAURA?
WHAT'S UP, WILLOW?

I'M NOT FEELING VERY WELL...
CAN I SIT THIS ACTIVITY OUT?
DO YOU WANT TO GO TO THE NURSE?
NO!
NO...
I'M NOT THAT SICK...
I'M JUST NOT FEELING WELL ENOUGH TO...
RUN AROUND AND STUFF.
YOU DON'T HAVE TO DO ANYTHING YOU DON'T WANT TO DO.
IF YOU'RE REALLY NOT FEELING WELL, YOU CAN SIT AND HELP ME KEEP SCORE.

C'MON, WILLOW!
HAVE A TURN!
NO, THANKS.

OH, DO YOU GUYS WANT TO SIT WITH MY ACTING GROUP?
SURE!

COME ON, WILLOW.
CAN'T YOU SIT WITH ME INSTEAD?
WE CAN ALL SIT TOGETHER...
I DON'T WANT TO SIT WITH MAX'S FRIENDS. OR ANYONE.
YOU SPENT ALL DAY HANGING OUT WITH OTHER PEOPLE. CAN'T WE EAT DINNER AT OUR OWN TABLE?
OKAY...

SIGH.

OLIVE!
COULD YOU DO MY HAIR FOR THE DANCE? YOU DID SUCH A NICE BRAID LAST TIME.
SURE!

WILLOW, COULD YOU COME HERE?
DO YOU WANT TO BORROW ONE OF MY HAIR CLIPS? I THINK IT WOULD LOOK REALLY NICE WITH YOUR DRESS.
...OKAY.

C'MON, GUYS!
LET'S GET THERE BEFORE THE ICE CREAM LINE GETS TOO LONG!
I LIKE YOUR DRESS, WILLOW.
...THANKS.

HEY!
HEY, MAX.
YOU REMEMBERED TO PACK A NICE SHIRT THIS YEAR!
YEAH, I HAD TO GET ONE FOR MY SCHOOL CHOIR CONCERT SO I FIGURED WHY NOT PACK IT, RIGHT?

DOES IT LOOK DUMB?
NO! IT LOOKS GOOD.
YEAH, I LIKE IT.
A LOT OF THE OTHER GUYS IN MY BUNK DIDN'T EVEN GET CHANGED...
I WISH FEWER OF THE GIRLS IN OUR BUNK DRESSED UP.
THERE WERE TEN OF US AND ONLY TWO MIRRORS IN THE BATHROOM.
I HOPE THEY PLAY THAT NEW CRYSTAL GIRLS SONG.
THE ONE WITH THE MUSIC VIDEO THAT'S SET IN OUTER SPACE?
OOOOH! I LIKE THAT ONE!
UMM... OLIVE?

WHAT'S UP, MAX?
I WAS WONDERING...
IF THE NEXT SONG IS GOOD...
WOULD YOU WANT TO DANCE WITH ME?
I... UMM...
OKA—
NO.
WHA—
NO!

IS EVERYTHING OKAY?
NO.
OLIVE WANTS TO ABANDON ME AGAIN TO GO DANCE WITH MAX.
ABANDON YOU?
IT WOULD JUST BE ONE DANCE WITH MAX AND THEN I'LL DANCE WITH YOU, OKAY?
AND WHAT AM I SUPPOSED TO DO WHILE YOU'RE GONE?!

YOU COULD DANCE WITH ME WHILE OLIVE DANCES WITH MAX.
C'MON, IT'LL BE F—
NO!
WHATEVER!
FORGET IT!
DO WHAT YOU WANT!
WILLOW...
WILLOW! WAIT!

WHAT IS GOING ON WITH YOU?
YOU'RE...
YOU'RE SUPPOSED TO BE MY FRIEND.
I AM YOUR FRIEND.
IF YOU'RE MY FRIEND THEN WHY DO YOU ALWAYS WANT TO HANG OUT WITH OTHER PEOPLE?

I DON'T ALWAYS HANG OUT WITH OTHER PEOPLE.
WE SPEND A TON OF TIME TOGETHER.
THEN WHY DOES IT FEEL LIKE YOU'RE ALWAYS LEAVING ME ALONE?!
I HAVE OTHER FRIENDS.
I CAN'T SPEND EVERY SECOND WITH YOU.
AND MAYBE IF YOU HAD **ANY** OTHER FRIENDS YOU WOULDN'T NEED ME TO!

WILLOW, I DIDN'T ME—
IT'S FINE.
I'D RATHER HAVE NO FRIENDS THAN A FRIEND WHO DOESN'T WANT ME.
SNIP

CLINK!
FINE.

IS THIS WHAT YOU WANT?
SNIP!

WILLOW?! WAIT!

NOPE,
NOPE,
NOPE.
YOU'RE NOT RUNNING OFF TOO.
BUT–
JUST LET LAURA HANDLE IT, OKAY?

YAWN
G'MORNING.

YOUR COUNSELORS WILL BE HANDING OUT SIGN-UP FORMS FOR THIS WEEK'S ACTIVITIES. THE PROCESS IS THE SAME AS LAST TIME.
IF THERE'S ANYTHING YOU WANT TO SIGN UP FOR, DO IT NOW OR YOU'LL BE WAITING UNTIL NEXT SUMMER!
IS IT OKAY IF I DROP MAGIC SO I CAN TAKE SKATEBOARDING THIS WEEK?
WHATEVER.

HEY, GUYS, MAX WAS JUST TELLING ME ABOUT AN IDEA FOR A VIDEO.
I WAS THINKING WE COULD BUILD ONE OF THOSE THINGS WITH THE CHAIN REACTION—
YOU KNOW—WITH THE DOMINOES AND STUFF—
A RUBE GOLDBERG MACHINE!
YEAH, THAT'S IT!
AND WE CAN MAKE IT OUT OF STUFF FROM AROUND CAMP AND—

WHERE ARE YOU GOING?
DON'T YOU WANNA HELP?
I'M NOT TAKING VIDEO THIS WEEK.
OH... OKAY.
WE SHOULD PROBABLY START COLLECTING SUPPLIES AND THEN FIGURE OUT WHAT TO DO WITH THEM AFTER.
LAURA SAID WE COULD WORK ON IT FOR TWO HOURS IF WE SKIP PAINTING.

DOMINOES

QUITE THE IMPRESSIVE CONTRAPTION YOU HAVE GOING ON...
BUT IF YOU WANT TO SET IT OFF YOU'D BETTER GET TO IT.
WE'RE CHANGING ACTIVITIES IN TEN MINUTES.
CAN'T WE LEAVE IT SET UP AND FILM IT TOMORROW?
I'M SORRY, GUYS, BUT OTHER PEOPLE NEED TO USE THE ART BARN AND IT TAKES UP TOO MUCH SPACE.
IT'S OKAY. WE'RE ALMOST READY, RIGHT?
YEAH, WE JUST NEED TO GET THE VIDEO CAMERA GOING.

NO PROBLEM, JUST LET ME–
OH...YES PROBLEM.
I MAY HAVE FORGOTTEN TO CHECK TO SEE IF THE CAMERA WAS CHARGED.
IT'S OKAY!
WE JUST NEED TO RUN AND GET A FRESH BATTERY FROM THE TECH SHED!

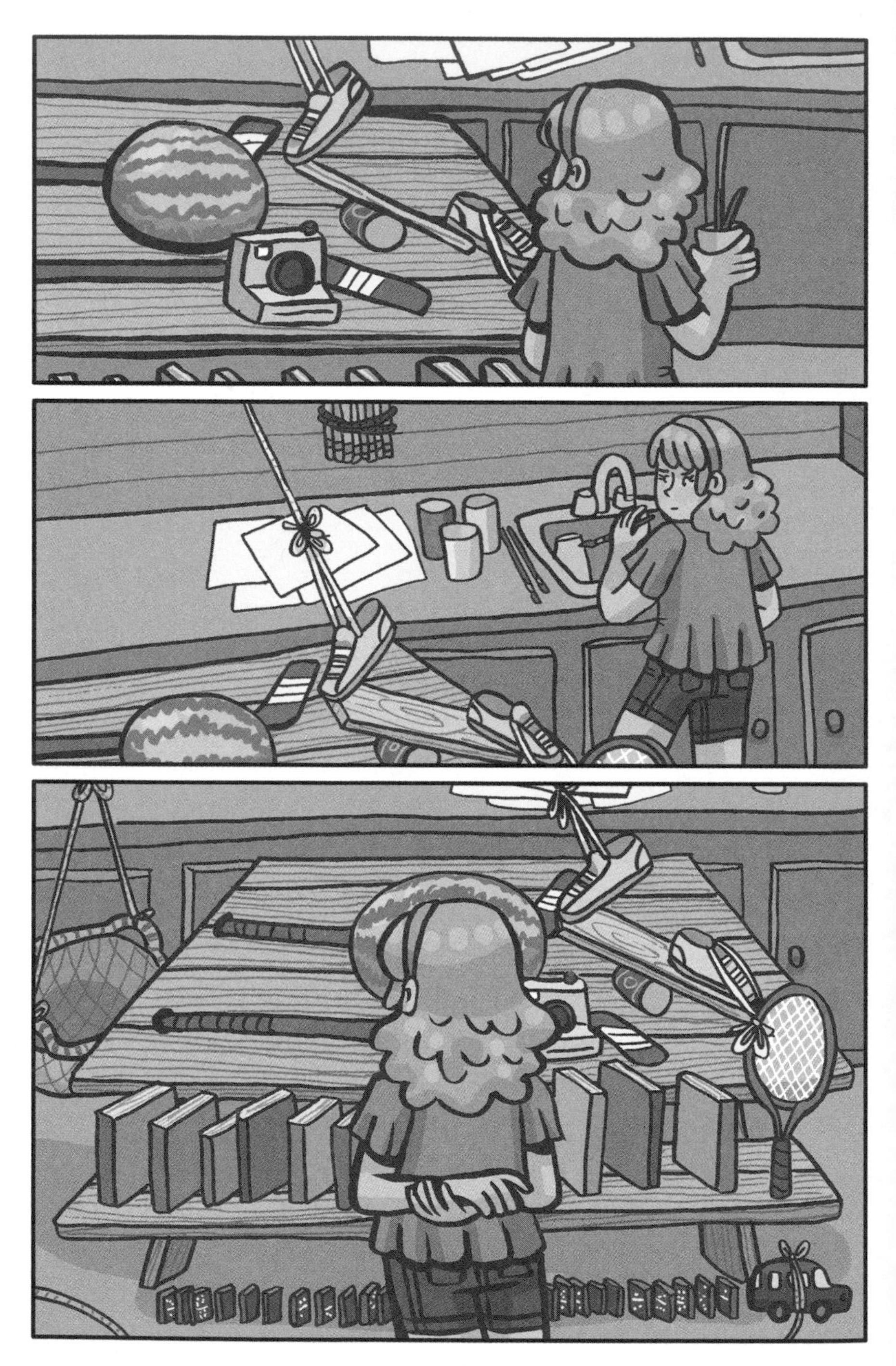

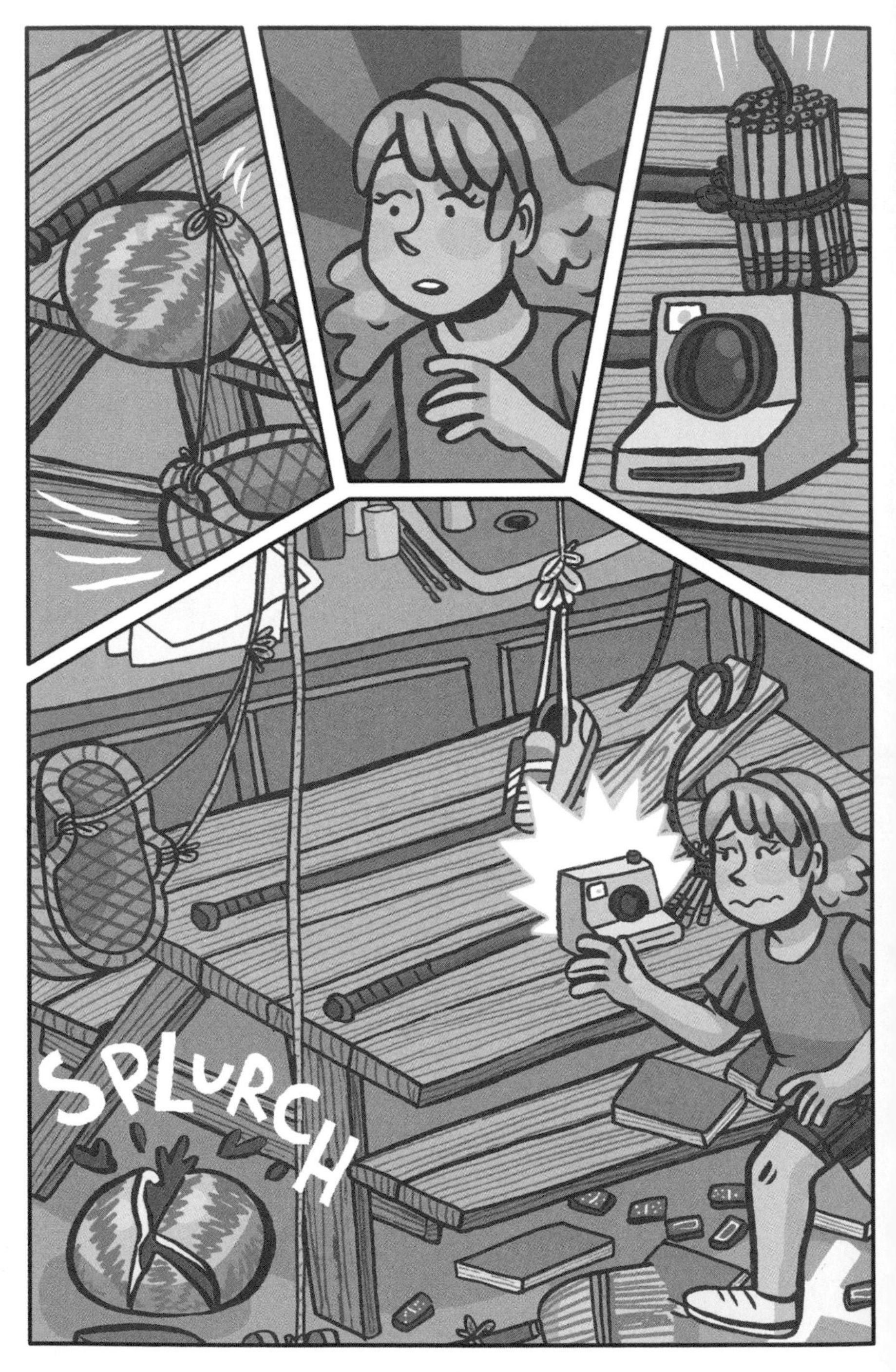
SPLURCH

WE STILL HAVE FIVE MINUTES—THAT SHOULD BE LONG ENOUGH TO—

SOMETHING MUST HAVE... SET IT OFF.
CAN WE REBUILD IT?
WE'LL NEED TO FIND SOMETHING TO USE INSTEAD OF THE WATERMELON.
I HAD A HARD ENOUGH TIME CONVINCING THE CHEF TO GIVE ME THE FIRST ONE.
A BASKETBALL WOULD BE THE RIGHT SIZE, BUT NOT HEAVY ENOUGH TO LIFT THE WEIGHT...
TOO BAD THERE ARE NO BOWLING BALLS AT CAMP.

GUYS! LOOK...
SHE DID THIS! SHE RUINED OUR RUBE GOLDBERG MACHINE BECAUSE SHE'S MAD AT ME.
AT LEAST SHE WON'T GET AWAY WITH IT— WE HAVE PROOF.
COME ON, LET'S GO TELL LAURA!
I DON'T KNOW, OLLIE... SHE'S BEEN HAVING A ROUGH TIME, RIGHT?
YEAH, I'M UPSET... BUT I DON'T WANT TO GET HER IN TROUBLE.

I AT LEAST WANT TO LET **HER** KNOW THAT **WE** KNOW.
WILLOW, WE-
OH MY GOSH!

WHAT A MESS!
COULD YOU TRY TO GET THIS CLEANED UP BEFORE MOVING ON TO YOUR NEXT ACTIVITY?
OKAY, LAURA.
WE CAN STAY A LITTLE LATE IF WE NEED TO.
OLIVE, COULD YOU PLEASE COME HELP?
BUT... I... THE THING IS... IT'S–
OLIVE, PLEASE.

SIGH.

OKAY, SO TODAY ON OUR WALK WE'RE GOING TO PARTNER UP AND TRY TO FIND LEAVES FROM FIVE DIFFERENT KINDS OF TREES. WE'RE AN ODD NUMBER, SO WE EITHER NEED A GROUP OF THREE OR SOMEONE CAN BE MY BUDDY FOR THE DAY.
I'LL BE YOUR PARTNER!
AWESOME! THAT'S SETTLED, THEN.
C'MON, EXPLORERS!
ARE YOU OKAY, OLLIE?
HUH?

YOU'RE BEING REALLY QUIET.
OH... SORRY. I'M JUST THINKING ABOUT WILLOW.
SHE'S ACTING WEIRD...AND KIND OF MEAN.
WELL, SHE'S BEEN ACTING "WEIRD AND KIND OF MEAN" TO ME SINCE WE GOT HERE.
YEAH... I GUESS... BUT WE'RE FRIENDS.
IF YOU'RE FRIENDS THEN SHE'LL GET OVER IT, RIGHT?
I HOPE SO...

WILLOW! WHERE ARE YOU GOING? SOFTBALL PRACTICE IS THIS WAY.
YEAH...AND MY DRUM LESSON IS THIS WAY.
COME ON.

SCIENCE
ART BARN

WOULD IT BE OKAY IF I SIT AT THE FERRET TABLE TODAY?
SORRY, WILLOW, WE HAVE TO SIT BY BUNKS.
PLEASE, PLEASE, PLEASE?
WE HAVE SOMETHING IMPORTANT TO DISCUSS.
YEAH, IT'S SUPER IMPORTANT AND WE PROMISE IT'S JUST THIS ONE TIME. PLEASE?

SO LONG AS JAY AND ADAM ARE OKAY WITH IT.
BUT THIS IS A ONE-TIME THING.

OH, OLIVE!
COULD YOU HELP ME TAKE THESE EMPTY EGG CARTONS OVER TO THE ART BARN? I NEED THEM FOR A CRAFT ACTIVITY TOMORROW.
EGGS
UMM, WELL— I WAS GOING TO... UH—
SURE, LAURA.
EGGS
EGGS

WHERE'S WILLOW?
SHE STOPPED AT THE CABIN TO CHECK IN, BUT THEN SHE WENT OUT AGAIN.
MAYBE SHE WENT TO THE MAIN OFFICE TO MAIL HER LETTERS AND POSTCARDS?
I'M GOING TO GO FIND HER.
OKAY, JUST BE BACK BY CURFEW.

CAN I HELP YOU WITH SOMETHING, DEAR?
NO, MA'AM...
I WAS JUST LOOKING FOR SOMEONE...

SIGH

Band practice
in Session!
Do NOT DISTURB!

TSSCH
BUMBUMBUH
BUHM
BAH
TSSCH

WHOA THERE, KIDDO.

GETTING TO ROAM AROUND DURING YOUR FREE TIME IS A PRIVILEGE AND A RESPONSIBILITY.
IF YOU ARE NOT RESPONSIBLE ENOUGH TO HANDLE IT, THE PRIVILEGE WILL BE TAKEN AWAY.
YEAH! IF YOU'RE LATE FOR CURFEW, YOU'LL HAVE TO SPEND THE REST OF YOUR FREE HOURS HERE WITH US...SORTING LAUNDRY! MWUHAHAHA!
I UNDERSTAND.
NOW GO GET READY FOR BED. IT'LL BE LIGHTS OUT BEFORE YOU KNOW IT.

BAH
BUM
BUM
Bah-
BRUM

KISSSH
BUHM
BRUMM
BUH-
BUM
BUH
DUM

BAH-KSSSH
TING
BUH-DUM
BRUM
BAH
KSSSH
BUHM
DA DUM
WILLOW!
BUH
WILLOW! LOOK AT ME!
BRUM

Bah-BRUM
BUH
DATDUM
PLEASE, WILLOW!
STOP!
WHY WON'T YOU LISTEN TO ME!?
WIL-
DUHM
WHOA!
KSSSHHTT'r

SIGH

WILLOW...
WILLOW, WAKE UP...
HUH?
I WANT TO TALK...
CAN WE GO OUTSIDE FOR A SECOND?
UMM...
OKAY. LET'S GO.

I'M
SORRY...

I...I SAW YOU GUYS HAVING FUN TOGETHER... AND I GOT JEALOUS.
I MESSED UP YOUR PROJECT ON PURPOSE.
BUT I DIDN'T REALIZE IT WOULD GET SO MESSED UP THAT YOU COULDN'T SET IT UP AGAIN TOMORROW!
THE ONLY PART THAT'S BROKEN-BROKEN IS THE WATERMELON.
I'M SURE WE'LL FIGURE OUT SOMETHING TO REPLACE IT EVENTUALLY...
SIGH
THAT'S NOT EVEN WHAT I'M UPSET ABOUT...

I'VE BEEN FEELING REALLY CRUDDY ALL DAY...
ABOUT OUR FIGHT...
ABOUT EVERYTHING.
BUT EVERY TIME I WANTED TO TALK TO YOU, YOU AVOIDED ME!
IT FELT LIKE NONE OF IT MATTERED TO YOU.
LIKE I DIDN'T MATTER TO YOU.
THAT'S HOW I'VE BEEN FEELING WATCHING YOU WITH ALL YOUR NEW FRIENDS.

I NEVER MEANT TO MAKE YOU FEEL THAT WAY.
I WISH YOU WOULD HAVE TOLD ME HOW YOU WERE FEELING BEFORE IT TURNED INTO A FIGHT.
ME TOO...
I KNOW I OVERREACTED...
I JUST DIDN'T EXPECT TO BE SO MISERABLE...
AND YOU'RE THE ONLY PERSON I KNOW HERE, SO I KIND OF LATCHED ON.

I'M SORRY I PUT SO MUCH PRESSURE ON YOU... IT WASN'T FAIR.
IT'S OKAY. I'M SORRY IF YOU FELT LIKE I WASN'T THERE FOR YOU.
IT'S OKAY.
I KNOW YOU TRIED.

NOW THAT WE'VE MADE UP, I WISH WE HADN'T CUT OFF OUR FRIENDSHIP BRACELETS.
YEAH, ME TOO.
SOOO...SINCE I SIGNED UP FOR A FEW ACTIVITIES WITHOUT YOU I WAS KINDA FORCED TO MEET SOME NEW PEOPLE...
A FEW OF THE KIDS AT THE TUNE SHACK ASKED ME TO BE IN THEIR BAND.
YEAH...I KIND OF PEEKED IN THE WINDOW WHEN YOU WERE REHEARSING THIS EVENING.

NEXT TIME WE PRACTICE, YOU SHOULD COME LISTEN FROM INSIDE THE SHACK.
WHAT KIND OF SONG—
OH THANK GOODNESS.
I WOKE UP AND SAW THAT YOU WEREN'T IN YOUR BEDS
AND YOU WEREN'T IN THE BATHROOM
AND I GOT SO SCARED!
I'M SO GLAD YOU'RE ALL RIGHT.
YOU **ARE** OKAY, RIGHT?
WHAT ARE YOU DOING UP?
AND OUTSIDE?
SHOULD I GET THE NURSE?

I HAD A NIGHTMARE AND IT WOKE ME UP.
SO WE CAME OUTSIDE TO TALK.
I FEEL A LOT BETTER NOW. I THINK I SHOULD BE ABLE TO FALL BACK ASLEEP.
GOOD. BECAUSE IT'S **WAY** PAST LIGHTS OUT.

NO

NO BAD

ACORN LAKE
HELLO
WHAT ARE YOU WORKING ON?
HUH?
YOUR DRAWING.
IT'S OF WILLOW.

WHOA,
WILLOW PLAYS THE DRUMS?
SHE JUST STARTED LEARNING, BUT SHE'S GETTING THE BASICS DOWN.
THAT'S AWESOME!
YEAH. I WAS WATCHING HER PRACTICE WITH A FEW OTHER KIDS AT THE TUNE SHACK YESTERDAY.
JAY HAS BEEN COACHING THEM AND THEY ACTUALLY SOUND PRETTY GOOD.
SO... WILLOW'S IN A BAND!? WE SHOULD TOTALLY MAKE A MUSIC VIDEO FOR THEM!
YEAH, THAT SOUNDS LIKE FUN.
JAY IS ONE OF MY BUNK COUNSELORS, SO I'LL ASK HIM ABOUT IT LATER.

HEY, GUYS!
JAY SAID HE'LL HELP WITH THE MUSIC VIDEO!
AWESOME!
MUSIC VIDEO?

I KIND OF TOLD MAX AND BREE ABOUT YOUR BAND.
AND WE THOUGHT IT WOULD BE FUN TO FILM YOU PLAYING.
YOU NEVER TOLD ANYONE AT THE BUNK YOU PLAYED IN A BAND!
WELL, IT'S NOT REALLY A BAND, AND I'M JUST LEARNING...
THAT'S STILL REALLY COOL!
I'D LOVE TO HELP YOU GUYS OUT WITH THE VIDEO.
YEAH! YOU CAN BE AN EXTRA!

I ALREADY TOLD THE OTHER KIDS IN THE BAND TO MEET US AT THE TUNE SHACK FOR FREE HOUR.
THANKS, JAY!
NO PROB.
SEE YA LATER.
MAX!
WAIT!

HUH?
I'VE BEEN THINKING...ABOUT THE RUBE GOLDBERG MACHINE YOU BUILT.
I THINK I KNOW HOW TO MAKE IT WORK WITHOUT THE WATERMELON.
I'M THINKING... SOFTBALLS?
hmmmm

ONE SOFTBALL WOULDN'T BE HEAVY ENOUGH TO LIFT THE WEIGHT.
FIG 1
FIG 2
AND I DON'T KNOW HOW WE'D GET MULTIPLE SOFTBALLS TO ROLL INTO THE BASKET AT ONCE.
FIG 1
FIG 2
BUT IF WE FILLED THE BASKET ALMOST ALL THE WAY, RIGHT TO THE TIPPING POINT, WE'D ONLY NEED TO ROLL ONE MORE SOFTBALL IN TO LIFT THE WEIGHT!
FIG 1
FIG 2

THAT SOUNDS LIKE IT MIGHT WORK!
I CAN GET US A WHOLE BUCKET OF SOFTBALLS FROM THE GYM!
WE COULD FILM IT AND USE THE FOOTAGE IN THE MUSIC VIDEO!
LAURA! CAN WE GO TO THE ART BARN AND REBUILD OUR MACHINE?
YEAH! PLEASE!
RIGHT NOW?
PLEASE please PLEASE PLEASE PLEASE
WELL...

I GUESS IF YOU FINISH ALL OF THE FOOD ON YOUR PLATES WE CAN LEAVE DINNER A LITTLE EARLY.
MUNCH NOM NOM
SCARF
HURRY UP SO WE CAN GO.
YOU WANT ME TO COME?
OF COURSE!
GULP MMM CHOMP MUNCH YUM

soup

IS EVERYONE READY?
YEAH!
I'LL START ROLLING THE CAMERA!
OKAY, HERE WE GO!
FLICK

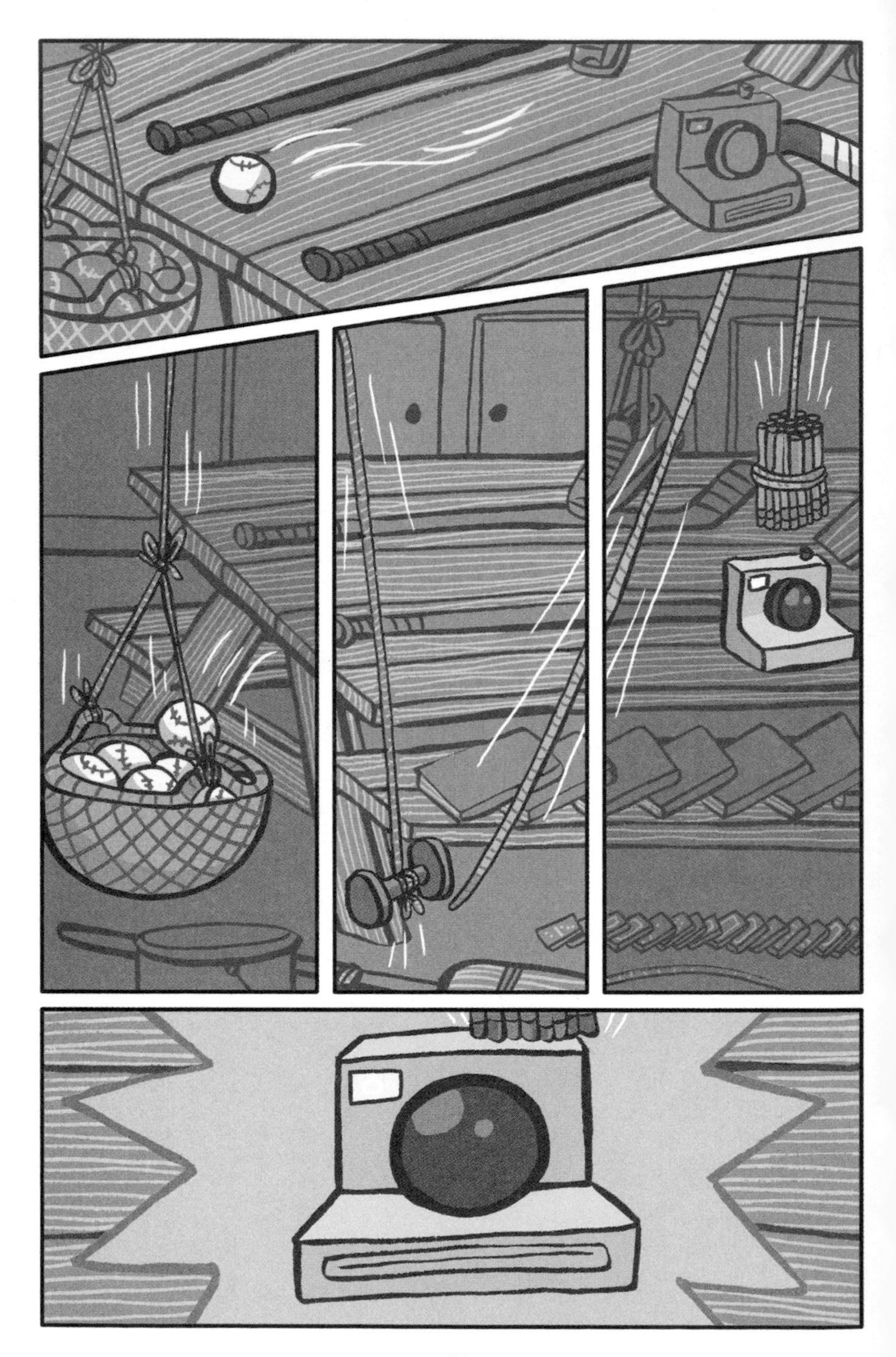

BZZZZT!
IT ACTUALLY WORKED!
LOOK, THE PHOTO IS DEVELOPING!
THAT WAS SO COOL! WE WOULDN'T HAVE BEEN ABLE TO DO IT WITHOUT YOU, WILLS!
WELL...TECHNICALLY YOU WOULD HAVE IF I HADN'T GOOFED WITH IT THE FIRST TIME YOU TRIED...

WE BETTER GET GOING TO THE TUNE SHACK!
WE'RE GOING TO BE LATE!
EXCUSE ME.
WHAT ABOUT THIS MESS?
CAN WE CLEAN UP IN THE MORNING?
PLEASE, LAURA, WE TOLD JAY WE'D MEET HIM FOR FREE HOUR.
SIGH.

I'LL TIDY UP AND PUT EVERYTHING TO THE SIDE...
BUT YOU GUYS ARE PUTTING ALL THIS STUFF BACK WHEREVER YOU TOOK IT FROM RIGHT AFTER BREAKFAST TOMORROW, OKAY?
THANK YOU, LAURA!
COME TO THE TUNE SHACK AFTER?
YOU CAN BE IN OUR VIDEO!
AND HEAR ME PLAY DRUMS!
YEAH, YEAH, NOW SCOOT BEFORE I CHANGE MY MIND ABOUT CLEANING UP AFTER YOU.

BREE,
OLIVE,
CHRIS...
MEET NOAH AND DYLAN.
EVERYONE ALREADY KNOWS MAX.
AND THIS IS MIA FROM CHIPMUNK BUNK.
AND OUR BAND NAME IS CHAIN REACTION!
WILLOW CAME UP WITH IT.
I HAD A LITTLE INSPIRATION...
IF EVERYONE IS ACQUAINTED LET'S GET STARTED.
WE'RE BURNING DAYLIGHT!

I CAN KEEP TWEAKING IT A LITTLE, BUT I THINK IT'S PRETTY MUCH DONE.
I THINK IT LOOKS GREAT, JAY.
WELL, THE KIDS GOT A LOT OF GREAT FOOTAGE. THE HARDEST PART WAS EDITING THINGS OUT.
ACORN LAKE

IT'S ALMOST CURFEW.
YEAH, WE SHOULD GET BACK TO THE BUNKS.
ONCE I FINISH EDITING, I'LL POST THE MUSIC VIDEO TO THE CAMP ACORN LAKE WEBSITE SO YOUR PARENTS CAN SEE IT.

STATE SCIENCE FAIR
I KNOW WE'RE ALL SAD ABOUT LEAVING TODAY...
BUT EVERYONE NEEDS TO CHEER UP FOR TEN SECONDS SO WE CAN TAKE A GROUP PICTURE!
LET'S GET SOMEONE FROM ANOTHER CABIN TO TAKE IT SO WE CAN ALL BE IN THE PICTURE, EVEN THE COUNSELORS!
23

OLLIE! WILLS!
COME STAND NEXT TO US!
OKAY!

CAMP ACORN LAKE
PUT YOUR PHONE NUMBER AND YOUR EMAIL DOWN!
I WANT TO INVITE EVERYONE TO MY BIRTHDAY PARTY THIS FALL!
AND PUT YOUR ADDRESSES IN MY NOTEBOOK SO I CAN SEND YOU GUYS PEN-PAL LETTERS!

OLIVE!
BREE!
WILLOW!
MAX!
I'M GLAD I FOUND YOU GUYS BEFORE YOU GOT ON THE BUS.

ARE YOU TWO COMING BACK NEXT YEAR?
I HOPE SO.
I HOPE SO TOO.
GIRLS, COME HERE!
MAX! C'MON, BUDDY!
IT WAS SO AMAZING TO MEET BOTH OF YOU.
I'M GOING TO MISS YOU, LAURA!
WILLOW, OLIVE, YOU'RE WITH ME.

CAMP ACORN LAKE
CAMP ACORN LAKE

I HOPE GOOBER DIDN'T MESS WITH MY STUFF WHILE WE WERE GONE...
I KNOW HE HAD HIS EYE ON THIS NEW PUZZLE I GOT FROM MY AUNT,
BUT I WANNA BUILD IT MYSELF FIRST BEFORE HE LOSES ANY OF THE—
SNIFF SNIFF
WHAT'S WRONG?
I JUST...
I'M JUST GOING TO MISS EVERYONE, YOU KNOW?
DON'T TELL ME YOU'RE GOING TO START FEELING HOMESICK FOR CAMP, TOO.

W ♥ O
O ♥ W

FOREVER
PM
Dear Olive,
Love,
Mom

WEEK TWO SCHEDULE
GOOD JOB!
Odds & ENDS

CAMP ACORN LAKE
OH NO!
LAKE SHARK!
SWIMMING AREA
DOCK
TUNE SHACK
BOATHOUSE
HELLO!
THEATER
MAX WUZ HERE!
So was BREE!
MAIL!
OFFICE
NO KIDS ALLOWED!
TENNIS COURTS
BASKETBALL COURT
STAFF CABINS
SOCCER FIELD

GIRL CABINS
OUR BUNK!
SHORTCUT
S'MORES IN ONE!
FIRE PIT
NATURE SHED
FOREST TRAIL
ROAR!
YUM!
BOY CABINS
MAX & JAY'S BUNK
MESS HALL
INFIRMARY
See you next summer! ♡ Chris
OUR DOMAIN! ♡♡
ACTION!
TECH + VIDEO
GYMNASIUM
ART BARN
SCIENCE + MAGIC
SOFTBALL FIELD
G + W 4 EVA!
SKATE PARK

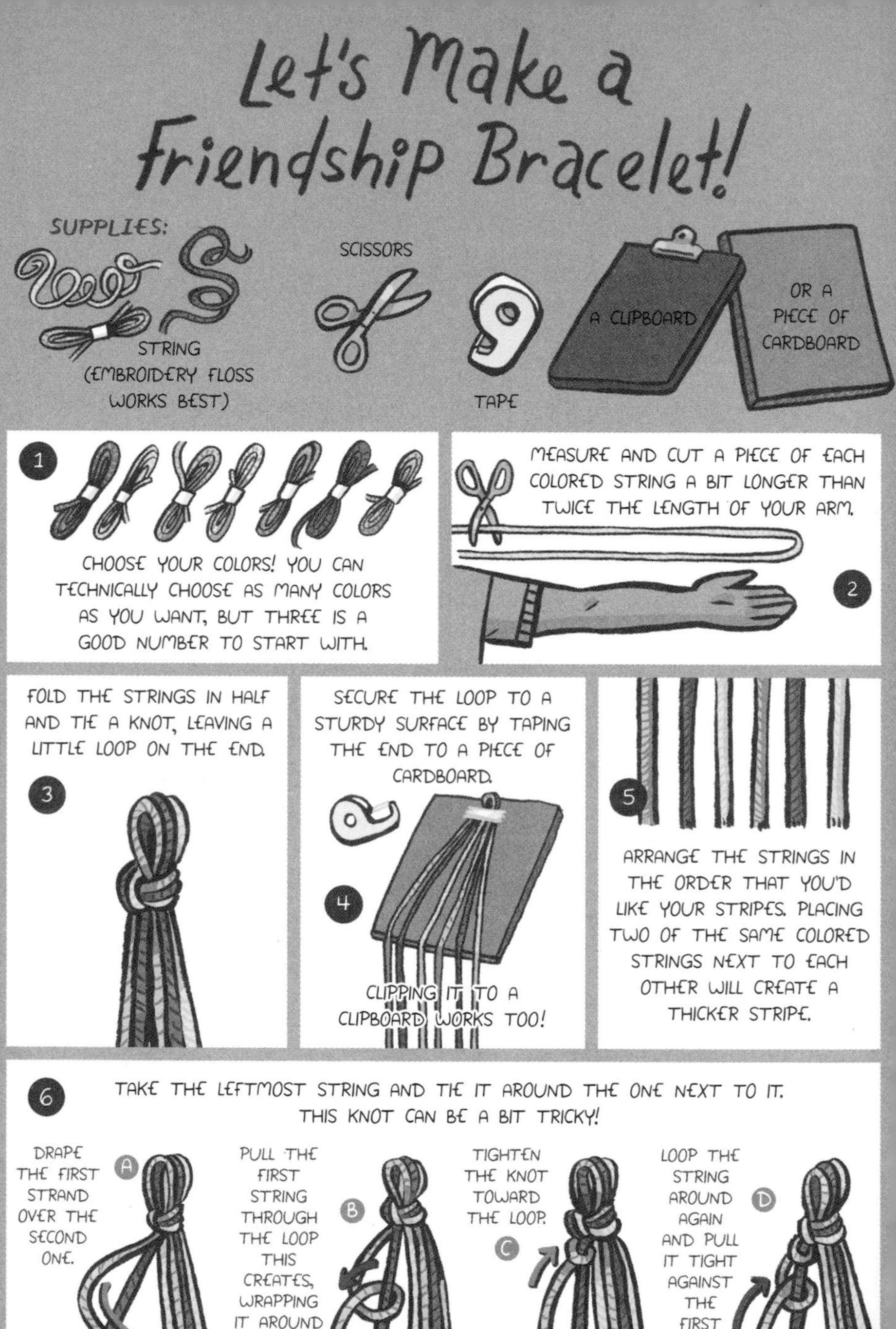
Let's Make a Friendship Bracelet!
SUPPLIES:
STRING (EMBROIDERY FLOSS WORKS BEST)
SCISSORS
TAPE
A CLIPBOARD
OR A PIECE OF CARDBOARD
1
CHOOSE YOUR COLORS! YOU CAN TECHNICALLY CHOOSE AS MANY COLORS AS YOU WANT, BUT THREE IS A GOOD NUMBER TO START WITH.
2
MEASURE AND CUT A PIECE OF EACH COLORED STRING A BIT LONGER THAN TWICE THE LENGTH OF YOUR ARM.
3
FOLD THE STRINGS IN HALF AND TIE A KNOT, LEAVING A LITTLE LOOP ON THE END.
4
SECURE THE LOOP TO A STURDY SURFACE BY TAPING THE END TO A PIECE OF CARDBOARD.
CLIPPING IT TO A CLIPBOARD WORKS TOO!
5
ARRANGE THE STRINGS IN THE ORDER THAT YOU'D LIKE YOUR STRIPES. PLACING TWO OF THE SAME COLORED STRINGS NEXT TO EACH OTHER WILL CREATE A THICKER STRIPE.
6
TAKE THE LEFTMOST STRING AND TIE IT AROUND THE ONE NEXT TO IT. THIS KNOT CAN BE A BIT TRICKY!
A
DRAPE THE FIRST STRAND OVER THE SECOND ONE.
B
PULL THE FIRST STRING THROUGH THE LOOP THIS CREATES, WRAPPING IT AROUND THE SECOND STRING.
C
TIGHTEN THE KNOT TOWARD THE LOOP.
D
LOOP THE STRING AROUND AGAIN AND PULL IT TIGHT AGAINST THE FIRST KNOT.

7
USING THE STRING THAT WAS ORIGINALLY ON THE LEFT, YOUR FIRST STRING, AND REPEAT THE PROCESS OF TYING IT AROUND THE REST OF THE STRINGS UNTIL YOU GET TO THE END OF THE LINE. THIS IS YOUR FIRST STRIPE!
8
TAKE THE STRING THAT'S NOW THE FURTHEST TO THE LEFT AND REPEAT THE PROCESS OF KNOTTING IT AROUND THE OTHER STRINGS, JUST AS YOU DID WITH YOUR FIRST STRING...
9
...AND THEN DO THIS AGAIN AND AGAIN AND AGAIN...
UNTIL THE BRACELET IS AS LONG AS YOU WANT IT TO BE.
10
TIE OFF THE END. SOME PEOPLE LIKE TO DO A LITTLE BRAID BEFORE TYING A KNOT IN THE END. THIS ISN'T NECESSARY, BUT IT IS CUTE AND CAN MAKE IT EASIER TO UNTIE IF YOU WANT TO TAKE IT OFF.
11
TO FASTEN, PULL THE STRINGS (OR THE BRAID) AT THE FINISHED END OF THE BRACELET THROUGH THE LOOP YOU CREATED AT THE BEGINNING AND TIE IT!

What Is a Rube Goldberg Machine?

A Rube Goldberg Machine is a contraption created to complete a simple task in an unnecessarily complicated and impractical way, often through a comical chain reaction. These mechanisms are named after the cartoonist and inventor Rube Goldberg who illustrated many such machines throughout his career, popularizing them in his comic strip **The Inventions of Professor Lucifer Gorgonzola Butts**. Most of his cartoon creations wouldn't have worked due to their complexity, frequent use of unpredictable live animals to trigger parts of the sequences, and general silliness...but they were so amusing that they inspired generations of people to create their own Rube Goldberg Machines—some of which **do** work!

Rube Goldberg Machines have a history of being featured in films-usually making breakfast, for some reason. There is even an annual contest where students from around the United States build their own themed Rube Goldberg Machines designed to complete a mundane task, such as sharpening a pencil or shutting off an alarm clock, in no fewer than twenty steps.

The photo-taking machine Olive and her friends build in this book only has ten steps...and is, at the point this is being written, COMPLETELY untested.

Acknowledgments

Shout-out to my camp family, especially my amazing co-counselors Andy and Yael, the Bolnick family, my snack-pack pal Kimber, my campers, and everyone from the Art Barn! I may not have spent a lot of time at camp, but it was a...formative experience.

I'd also like to thank everyone at HMH for their enthusiasm for **Click** and **Camp!** I am still amazed that anyone let me make a book-nevermind TWO books! I'm so grateful to Mary, Andrea, and Alia for all of your support.

And, of course, MUCH thanks to my agent neé editor, Elizabeth, without whom Olive wouldn't exist.

Last, but certainly not least, thank you to my friends and family! Mom, Dad, Grandma, and Grandpa-for always supporting me and never getting annoyed at me for working on my laptop during family gatherings. Miguel-for everything, including your help coloring this book. Christine and Patch-for your advice. K and Will-for listening to me ramble and gripe. And my Jeffrey-for being my proofreader, sounding board, cheerleader, voice of reason, and dear friend.

-KAYLA